Bringing the past to life, warts and all!

Toffs and Toshers

Dad's getting on his soapbox now. "And Rent-a-Rabble are *privileged* to play The People Who Time Forgot. We Tell It Like It Was! Would you believe it, kids? Some of those poor wretches in Victorian times were reduced to collecting dog dirt! It was used in the tanning industry to darken leather. And they only got a penny a sack!"

"Did they, Dad?" says Rupert, his eyes gleaming. Rupert loves anything disgusting. "Did they really collect dog dirt? Can I be a dog-dirt collector, Dad? Can I? Can I? Do I need a shovel?"

Look out for more books in this revolting
series. . .

THE REVOLTING RABBLES

Bringing the past to life, warts and all!

Toffs and Toshers

SUSAN GATES

Illustrated by Leo Broadley

SCHOLASTIC

Scholastic Children's Books,
Commonwealth House, 1-19 New Oxford Street,
London, WC1A 1NU, UK
a division of Scholastic Ltd
London ~ New York ~ Toronto ~ Sydney ~ Auckland
Mexico City ~ New Delhi ~ Hong Kong

First published in the UK by Scholastic Ltd, 2002

ISBN 0 439 99441 1

Typeset by M Rules
Printed by Cox & Wyman Ltd, Reading, Berks.

10 9 8 7 6 5 4 3 2 1

To my own rabble of a family –
Laura, Alex, Chris and Phil.

Chapter One

"Guess what, kids? We've got our next job!"

Dad's just come bouncing into the kitchen. He's waving a letter about. And he's beaming all over his face.

"Oh, yeah?" I don't want to be a party-pooper. But I've only just recovered from our last job. It takes a long time to live down being an Elizabethan Bearded Lady.

"You know that Victorian street they've built right inside the City Museum?" asks Dad. "That's got shops and houses just like the real thing? Well, they're going to fill it with a big crowd of Victorian characters just for one day. And, guess what, they've hired us to be part of it."

"Cool!" shouts my little brother, Rupert. "Can we choose which Victorian characters we're going to be, Dad?"

"*Er*, within limits, son."

Why does Rupert even bother asking? He knows the rules. He *knows* we can't choose to be anyone important or powerful. You only have to look at the new snappy slogan that's painted on our van: "WE NEVER PLAY PRINCES. WE ARE PROUD TO PLAY PEASANTS AND PAUPERS!"

In case you haven't heard of us, we're Rent-a-Rabble, the real history people. You can look us up on our web site. We hire ourselves out for historical events. But we only ever play poor, downtrodden people like serfs or servants or slaves.

"And, of course, we'll have to do some research," Dad replies to Rupert. "To make sure we're absolutely authentic. We must get the details right."

Dad's painted that on our van too: "THE DRAMA'S IN THE DETAIL".

When our van passes by people read our slogans, scratch their heads and say, *"What's that all about then?"*

"But trust me," Dad rambles on, "you'll be spoiled for choice. The streets were swarming with poor, hungry, homeless people in Victorian times. People who shuffled around barefoot in rags and lived crowded into damp, stinking hovels."

"Wait a minute," I interrupt him. "That sounds familiar. Isn't that just like the peasants we played in our medieval job?"

But Dad doesn't get sarcasm; he never jokes about history.

"That's a very wise observation, Rae," he tells me, nodding gravely. "It's hundreds of years later. But poor people's lives haven't changed much."

So we're wearing brown rags again. Can't we wear shoes just once?

But I feel selfish and heartless when Dad cries, "Yes, they are still suffering!"

"Still suffering, Dad," repeats Rupert, like a parrot. Rupert can be such a creep.

Dad's getting on his soapbox now. "And Rent-a-Rabble are *privileged* to play The People Who Time Forgot. We Tell It Like It Was! Would you believe it, kids? Some of those poor wretches in Victorian times were reduced to collecting dog dirt! It was used in the tanning industry to darken leather. And they only got a penny a sack!"

"Did they, Dad?" says Rupert, his eyes gleaming. Rupert loves anything disgusting. "Did they really collect dog dirt? Can I be a dog-dirt collector, Dad? Can I? Can I? Do I need a shovel?"

Dad doesn't seem to hear Rupert's questions. He's not in the modern world. His eyes are dreamy and far away. He's back in Victorian times. "And others," he continues, sorrowfully, "sat in sewers and sieved through human excrement. To find rings or coins that rich people had dropped down drains. They were called *toshers*—"

"Rupert!" warns Mum, who's passing through the kitchen. She's wearing her smart black business suit and carrying her laptop

4

computer. "If you lay one finger on my kitchen sieve, I'll kill you!"

"Excellent, Mum!" says Rupert, looking delighted. "Threaten me some more. Go on, *really* tell me off. Because Victorian parents were dead strict."

Mum mutters something like, "You can never win!" then slams the door behind her. She's late for the office.

"Where's Ryan?" asks Dad, looking round. "Time to do some research, kids. Surf the net. Visit the library. Let's get into the Victorian mood!"

Right on cue my big brother Ryan, the gadget freak, drifts into the kitchen. He pours himself some juice. He doesn't notice us. He's on another planet as usual, thinking about inventions.

Rupert says, "I'm going to be a Victorian dog-dirt collector, bro'!" like he wants Ryan to say, "Congratulations!"

And Ryan *does* turn round. It's amazing. He's actually reacting!

"The Victorians!" he says, sounding thrilled. "Is that our next job? That's The Great Age of Invention! They invented electric lights, telephones, photography, railways. It was really exciting. . ."

He drifts out of the kitchen. We can hear him rabbiting on about Victorian inventions all the way up the stairs, "Safety pins and chocolate bars and Christmas crackers and chewing gum and zip fasteners. . ."

Just before we go to the library, I spy Rebel, our historical hound, in the garden. "Rebel's back," I tell Dad. We're all pleased to see him. He's been gone three days. Don't ask where – Rebel always has his reasons.

Rupert's out in the garden too. He's creeping round after Rebel with a supermarket carrier bag and a shovel. Rebel looks behind him. He raises his bushy white eyebrows at me, as if to say, "What's this lunatic up to now?"

What can I say? I mouth through the window, "He's just getting in the Victorian mood!"

Chapter Two

We're in the Rent-a-Rabble van, on our way back from the library. I've been flicking through books, looking at old photos. But I still can't decide which character I'm going to play on Victorian Day.

Like Dad said, there's loads of choice. Loads of poor hungry children scrabbling for a living on Victorian streets. I could be a

Watercress Girl or a Match Seller. Or one of those kids who sold used tea leaves they found in rich people's rubbish.

How about being a Used Tea Leaf Seller? I ask myself. Dad would approve. You can't get much more humble than that. Except maybe a tosher, one of those kids that sieved for coins in sewers.

I'm thinking about it as our ancient old van chugs along, when a voice like a foghorn nearly bursts my eardrums. It's Rupert.

"Well done, Dad!" he's yelling. "You're being really authentic, only driving at 12 mph. That was the speed limit in Victorian times, wasn't it, Dad, when cars were first invented?"

Dad grits his teeth. He looks in the mirror at the long queue of cars behind us, desperate to overtake. "I'm not being authentic, Rupert. This old rustbucket won't go any faster."

"Never mind, Dad. Guess what?" Rupert says, looking through the scribbly notes he did at the library. "I've found something really authentic that Rebel can be."

Rebel's staring out of the van windows,

checking out the lady dogs o.

He hears his name and turns r.

He means, "You talking to me?"

"You could be Greyfriars Bobby,"

tells him. "He was a really famous

When his master died the faithful Greyfriars

Bobby sat by his grave for, like, fourteen

years! Through rain and snow and bitter

winds." Rupert sniffs a big juicy sniff and

brushes away a tear. "Honest, it's such a sad

story; it's really got to me."

"*Ruff?*" barks Rebel again in astonish-

ment. He raises his bushy eyebrows at me.

As if to say, "Fourteen years? Through snow

and bitter winds? That Greyfriars Bobby

should get a life!"

Rupert consults his notes again. What a

swot. Always trying to get into Dad's good

books.

"And Rae could be a sunbeam."

"A what?" I don't think I heard right.

"The Victorians said girls should be sun-

beams," says Rupert. "They must never look

miserable."

"You're kidding me!"

"No! You've got to smile all the time and

be ever so sweet and kind. It'd be a really tough challenge—"

I leap at him, "Stop winding me up, you little—"

"Dad, Dad!" he shrieks. "Rae's trying to strangle me. And I'm just being authentic. I'm – *nurrrgh* –"

We're rolling very, very slowly into the supermarket car park. I forgot we had to pick up some things for tea. I let go of Rupert's throat. "Don't mention that word *sunbeam* again. Ever!"

We leave Rebel and Ryan in the van. Rebel's not allowed in the supermarket. And Ryan's too busy thinking about inventions to be any help.

As we get a trolley, Rupert's still babbling about what he wants to be on Victorian Day. He sounds dead excited. "I could be a dog-dirt collector, a tosher, or a crossing sweeper! They swept horse dung up, so people could cross the streets."

"Rupert! Isn't there anything you can be that doesn't involve dung?"

"Course, Rae," says Rupert. "Have I got a lady's hands?"

"Pardon?"

"'Cos if I've got tiny, ladylike hands I could be a brilliant pickpocket. Nicking gloves and handkerchiefs and stuff. Victorian criminals are dead interesting. Did you know they spoke a special back-to-front language?"

"Did they?"

"*Sey!* And, as well as that, this freaky scientist guy thought you could tell who was a criminal just by feeling the bumpy bits on their heads. I should think it works best with baldies, don't you? 'Cos it's hard to feel bumps through hair."

"I don't think it works at all. Sounds like a load of rubbish to me."

"*Woh od uoy wnok?*"

"Rupert," I tell him with my darkest glare. "Shut up. Don't start talking in that stupid back-to-front language. It's so cheesy."

Rupert puts out his tongue, then yells, "*Maebnus!*"

"Dad, he's saying sunbeam!" Honestly, Rupert's so childish. He's gone before I can even grab him.

I'm just choosing some chocolate chip

cookies when I hear an angry squawk over by the bacon counter. And another one by the fresh-baked bread. What's all that about?

And where's Dad gone with the trolley? But just as I'm wondering he comes trundling down the aisle. He looks puzzled. At first I don't pay much attention because Dad looks puzzled most of the time. Modern life doesn't suit him. He was born at least a hundred years too late.

"Rupert's behaving very strangely!"

So what's new? But when I trudge after Dad to see what Rupert's doing, even I have to gasp.

He's creeping up on a baby. A tiny, new baby in a buggy, with a baldy head. Its proud mummy is boasting to another lady: "Justin's the perfect baby. He's so good. He's angelic!"

Rupert tippy-toes up, his eyes gleaming. He runs his hands over Justin's bald bonce like he's doing an examination. He frowns, sternly.

"Rupert!" shouts Dad, skidding up beside him with the trolley.

"That baby is a criminal!" Rupert announces to Dad in his foghorn voice.

Justin's mum can't believe her ears.

"What did you say?"

"I said, your baby's a criminal," says Rupert, sounding full of confidence. "I can tell by his bumps."

"How DARE you!"

Right in front of our eyes, Justin's mum turns into a fierce tigress. Fiery sparks seem to spit from her eyes. Even Rupert looks a bit worried.

She's quivering with rage. "Did you hear what he said!" she's saying as a group of mums gather around her. "About my innocent little angel?"

"He said it about my angel too!"

"And mine!"

"And about me!" adds another insulted voice. "And I'm a vicar!"

Oh, no. Rupert's been prowling around the supermarket, checking baldies' bumps. If that angry mob of mums get their hands on him, he's dog meat. Not to mention the mad vicar.

But Dad's already yanking Rupert down the aisle. "Sorry, sorry, sorry," he's apologizing.

As Dad frogmarches Rupert past the freezers, there's a guy bending down, looking in. He's got tree-trunk legs, rippling muscles, a tattoo that says "HATE" and a big, shiny, shaved bald head.

"Wait, Dad!" Rupert's fingers are itching.

"Don't even think about it!" With one mighty heave, Dad hurls Rupert out of the exit.

We hurry back to the van. Dad keeps glancing back over his shoulder. But no one's screaming for Rent-a-Rabble's blood. Dad looks surprised.

"*All* those babies in there were criminals," announces Rupert. "Isn't that an amazing coincidence?"

I narrow my eyes. I scowl suspiciously at him. Is he the world's biggest idiot? Or the world's biggest troublemaker? I can never make up my mind.

Dad's parking the van in our drive when I tell him, "Someone's left a big parcel by our back door."

"Excellent!" says Dad, leaping out. "I was expecting that. The museum where I used to work has loaned me some costumes.

Now we can really get stuck into this Victorian job. There'll be some ladies' costumes for you, Rae," he says. "They might help you make up your mind what you want to be."

"She could wear a bustle," booms Rupert so the whole street can hear. "That's padding that makes your bum look big. It was all the rage in Victorian times."

"Wait a minute," I say, warily. "Do you mean that Victorian ladies actually *wanted* their bums to look big?"

"Yeah," says Rupert. "The bigger the better."

Ryan snaps out of his daydream. "If you want a really big bum," he says, "what about a blow-up one? It would be dead easy to invent."

"No, no, no!" I've had enough of Ryan's inflatable inventions. I'm still cringing from that Elizabethan job, when he made Dad that pair of blow-up calves out of whoopee cushions. Don't ask me what happened. It's too painful to think about.

Ryan shrugs. "Your loss," he says. He's already heading for the garage where he makes most of his gadgets. "I'm going to be too busy anyway. I'm making a railway. The Victorian Age was the Golden Age of railways."

"That's true, son," agrees Dad. "But making a railway? Isn't that a bit ambitious?" Ryan just drifts away. He's not even listening.

Dad lugs the parcel of costumes into the house. "We'll unpack them tomorrow," he says. "Maybe we've had enough of the Victorians for one day."

He looks accusingly at Rupert.

"*Tnod emalb em,*" says Rupert.

"What?" says Dad, bewildered.

"Don't take any notice of him, Dad!" I tell him. "He's just winding you up, talking backwards language."

But instead of getting mad, Dad pats Rupert on the head. Rupert smiles at me, smugly.

"Very authentic, Rupert," Dad says. "Some of the Victorian criminal underworld did speak such a language. *Llew enod!*"

See, the two of them are at it now. That's what I have to put up with. Rebel and me are the only sane ones in a family of loonies. Plus Mum, of course. She's can't be loony. She's an accountant.

"There's no way I'm wearing a blow-up bum," I warn Dad in case he's forgotten.

I don't know why I'm worrying. I won't get to put on a fashionable lady's clothes anyway. I'll never be a princess, a queen or even a posh person.

"Just give us the scratchy, brown peasant costumes with holes for arms and legs. The ones that looks like coal sacks," I tell Dad, with a sigh.

That's what I always seem to end up wearing, whatever period in history we play.

"Look on the bright side, Rae," says Dad. "We're getting well paid for this job. And you'll get your share."

I'm looking forward to that. I'm really broke at the moment.

"That's if everything goes according to plan," adds Dad.

But that's the whole problem. When did any of Rent-a-Rabble's jobs ever go according to plan?

Chapter Three

Something wakes me up from a bad dream. I was crying in the dark. It was stinking darkness. I was scared and I couldn't breathe. I'm still shaking. Was I a little sweeping boy forced up chimneys? Or a tosher in the sewers? Or a kid who slaved down the mines and hardly ever saw daylight?

Whoever I was, life for poor kids in Victorian times wasn't a load of laughs. I wish I'd never done that research yesterday. Everyone looks so grim in those Victorian photos. Didn't they ever have any *fun*?

"*Aaargh!*"

That's what woke me up. It sounds like a cry of pain. It seems to be coming from downstairs! I scramble out of bed.

Rupert's already heard it. He's clattering down the shadowy stairs in front of me. We skid into the kitchen.

The light's on. And there's Dad hopping around holding his foot.

"*Ow, ow, ow,*" he says. "I was just sneaking down for a midnight snack. And I trod on something spiny."

"Oh, no!" Rupert's face screws up as if he's in pain too. "You've trod on our historical hedgehog! You haven't hurt him, have you?"

I knew we had a historical hound. But a historical hedgehog? When did he join Rent-a-Rabble?

I stare in amazement at Rupert. "You're kidding me! A hedgehog?"

Rupert looks hurt. He sticks out his bottom lip. "I'm just being authentic, Rae. Those Victorian dudes did keep hedgehogs in their kitchens, didn't they, Dad? And the hedgehogs ran about at night killing bugs and crunching up cockroaches. I'm right, aren't I, Dad? Dad? Dad?"

"Yes, son," gasps Dad, trying not to grimace with pain. "Top marks for enthusiasm. The Drama's in the Detail."

A spiky brown ball comes shuffling across the kitchen floor. I open the back door and he trundles straight out.

"Hey, you're letting my historical hedgehog go," protests Rupert.

"He's better off in the garden, son," winces Dad. "Where he can be wild and free."

"I could be a cockroach cruncher, Dad," says Rupert. "Instead of the hedgehog. Did they have *human* cockroach crunchers in Victorian times? Course, I wouldn't *eat* 'em like hedgehogs do." Me and Dad both look relieved. "I'd have special cockroach crunching boots to stamp on 'em. . ."

Dad and me share a long-suffering look. "I thought you'd decided to be a crossing sweeper?" interrupts Dad, feebly. "I mean, I don't want to force you or anything. . ."

Ryan's wandered in: "Was that somebody screaming?"

He's just heard Dad talking about crossing sweepers. "Those brooms they used to sweep up horse dung were dead inefficient," he says. "I could really improve on those."

Dad looks worried. "Remember the principles of Rent-a-Rabble, Ryan. We Tell It Like It Was. Warts and all. Scabby sores and all. We aren't about improving on history. We're about—"

Oh, no. Haven't I heard all this before? Ryan's already drifted back to bed. But Rupert moves closer, until he's almost treading on Dad's toes. He's staring intently up at Dad's face. What's so fascinating? Then he suddenly shouts, "Dad! I nearly mistook your moustache for a furry caterpillar!"

Dad stops in mid-rant. He looks hurt. He tries to hide his moustache with his hand. Ever since he hit forty-five he's been touchy about his looks.

"You should shave it off," advises Rupert. "Else people will think, 'Why's that guy going round with a furry caterpillar stuck to his top lip? That's cruel!'"

"But Victorian ladies admired men with big, bushy moustaches," protests Dad. "They thought they made men look macho."

"Well, yours isn't macho!" laughs Rupert, who isn't famous for being tactful. "My belly button fluff is more macho than that!"

Dad looks totally disheartened. "I suppose I *could* shave it off," he says sadly.

"No, don't do that," Mum yawns, poking her head into the kitchen. "I agree with those Victorian women. I think a moustache makes a man look distinguished."

Instantly, Dad cheers up. "See," he says, fluffing up his tiny toothbrush moustache. "I told you they were a hit with the ladies."

Where's Mum been? She took her time. You'd think that hearing Dad scream she'd be out of bed like a rocket.

"What's all the row down here?" she says. "It's woken me up. And I've got an important breakfast meeting tomorrow."

She goes to close the back door. "What's that doing open?"

I've only just started to explain about the

historical hedgehog when she sees something else. There's a supermarket carrier bag standing just outside in the yard. "What's this doing here? What's in it?"

Why do mums ask so many questions? It's no wonder they find out things they really don't want to know.

"That's mine," says Rupert. He sounds proud. "It took me ages to collect it. Big dogs, little dogs. I been round that park three times!"

Mum steps outside in her slippers. Sleepily, she starts fumbling with the bit of string tied round the top. . .

"No!" I shout out a warning. "Please – leave that alone, Mum."

"But what's in it?"

"Trust me, Mum, you really, *really* don't want to know. . ."

"Rupert!" I shriek at him when Mum's gone back to bed. "What are you playing at? Mum nearly opened that bag! Every job we do, you always get carried away. You go right over the top. You just have to *pretend* to be a Victorian. You don't have to really do it!"

"But that's part of the fun," says Dad.

"Dad!" I'm angry with him now. "You shouldn't let Rupert get away with it. Look at the trouble he caused in that supermarket. Those mums were really on the warpath!"

To my amazement Rupert agrees with me. For once he doesn't defend Dad, his hero.

"Yes, Dad, you're too soft. Don't let me get away with it! Those Victorian dads didn't mess about. Their word was LAW! Their kids had to be OBEDIENT. Listen to this Victorian poem I copied down about a boy that disobeys his dad. This is what happens to him. Right?"

Rupert flips open his notebook and reads sternly:

"What heavy guilt upon him lies!
How cursed is his name!
The ravens shall pick out his eyes,
And eagles eat the same!"

Dad squirms round uneasily. "Oh, dear, that's a bit harsh," he says. "Couldn't they just stop his pocket money?"

"But you don't even do that, Dad," complains Rupert. "You don't do nothing! Those Victorian dads, they scared their kids silly. If they sucked their thumbs, their dads said, 'A Scissor Man will come tonight and chop 'em off!' Go on, Dad, scare me to death. Give me a really hard time!"

Dad sighs. He looks really apologetic. "I'm sorry, Rupert but it's just not ME. I think children respond best to praise. . ."

Rupert shakes his head sadly. "You're a big failure as a Victorian dad, Dad," he says, as he stomps back up to bed.

Dad looks depressed. "Don't worry, Dad," I tell him. "Loads of dads are a big disappointment to their kids." That doesn't seem to cheer him up much.

I microwave myself a midnight snack. On my way back to bed I catch Dad taking a look inside the parcel of costumes.

"It's the middle of the night, Dad. Leave those until morning."

He jumps up, looking guilty.

"You're right, Rae," he says. "I was just taking a quick peek. Actually, some of them are quite unsuitable. The people from the museum don't seem to have grasped what Rent-a-Rabble is all about. They've sent some costumes that only well-off, middle-class Victorian folk would wear. There's even a top hat in here! A rather fine one, in fact. Of course, I can't possibly wear it."

Mum pops her head over the banisters. "Did someone say top hat? That would really suit you, Richard."

"Do you really think so?" says Dad.

He looks pleased. I think his confidence needs boosting a bit, after Rupert said he wasn't strict enough.

"They go so well with a really macho moustache," says Mum, as she disappears into the bedroom.

"Oh," says Dad, looking crushed again.

When I'm climbing the stairs, carrying my box of crinkle-cut chips, Dad's having another crafty peek in that parcel.

Chapter Four

Bong! Bong!

I've woken up again. It's daylight this time. My head's ringing. Who's making that dreadful din?

"Will you stop that!" I scream from under the duvet.

Bong! The whole house is shaking.

"Breakfast is served!" Rupert's voice

booms up the stairs. *Bong!* The air's trembling from the echoes. *BONG, bong, bong.*

It's no use, I can't stand it, I'll have to get up. I lean over the banisters.

"What's that terrible racket? It's making my teeth ache!"

"It's my gong!" Rupert shrieks back. "Want to hear it again?"

"No, *please!*" My ears are still buzzing.

"Victorian servants had to bang gongs in posh houses, to let rich people know their meals were ready," Rupert informs me smugly.

"Were they all as loud as that?" If they were, all rich Victorians must have been deaf.

"Er, no," confesses Rupert. "Ryan modified this one a bit. Look, it's wired up to his stereo speakers. No one's gonna miss breakfast with my gong!"

Oh, no, Ryan's started already, making gadgets, improving on history. Dad isn't going to like this one bit.

Rupert lifts up his little hammer. He's always liked bashing things, ever since he was a baby.

"Don't you dare!" It's too early in the morning to start being Victorian. It's too early to get out of bed. "It's the summer holidays!" I tell Rupert. "Don't you dare wake me up before lunch time."

"You've got to get up," says Rupert, sternly. "Or I'll report you to The Early Rising Society and you'll get fined."

"Fined? What are you talking about? I've never heard of this stupid Early Rising Society."

"The Victorians started it. The Early Rising Society didn't approve of people getting up late. Actually, I'm a member of it," says Rupert, piously. "I won't get fined. I've been up since six o'clock."

"Is there anything the Victorians *did* approve of?"

"They didn't like girls having their hair in fringes, for a start," says Rupert, giving me an accusing look.

"Come on, you're kidding me!" I push my fringe out of my eyes. "So what could girls do that they did approve of?"

"Embroidery," says Rupert. "You couldn't get into much trouble for doing that."

"Oh, great!" Why am I having this stupid conversation, hanging over a banister? "I'm going back to bed," I tell Rupert.

But first, I have to go to the bathroom.

Hang on! I know I'm still sleepy but what's going on? Where's the toilet? It used to be in that corner, I'm sure it did. Now all I can see is a mass of pink paper frills, like a ballet dancer's tutu.

"Rupert!" I roar. "What have you done to our toilet?"

"I've disguised it!" A smug voice comes floating up the stairs. "That's what the Victorians did. They always disguised anything embarrassing."

"But I can't even find it!"

"I read about it in this book," Rupert yells. "Victorians were very easily shocked. They even put frills on piano legs."

I've woken up in a madhouse. "I'm going to tell Dad what you've done!" I shout back.

"I'm only being authentic!"

"No, you're not, you're being awkward. Just to get on my nerves."

He shoots off, sniggering, before I can grab him.

I'm on my way downstairs to tell Dad when I bump into Ryan.

"Have you seen what Rupert's done?" I point furiously back to the bathroom. "This stupid frilly toilet! I can't even find the lid!"

Ryan says, "You upset about something, Rae?" Then he drifts off. His brain's full of inventions. There's no use trying to get any sense out of him.

Where's Rebel? I need to talk to Rebel. He'll reassure me I'm not going completely round the bend.

I go down to the kitchen.

"*Olleh*," says Rupert. I'm just summoning up the energy to thump him, when I see the carrots. They're arranged in a neat row on the table.

"Pink, frilly *vegetables*?" I comment, gritting my teeth.

"Of course," says Rupert, in a priggish voice. "I had to disguise them. So no one got shocked. That carrot was a very rude shape. It looked like a—"

"I don't want to know," I say, pushing my way past him. It'll only encourage him.

Rebel's not around. Nor is Mum, the other sane person in the family. She probably went to work hours ago.

"Where's Dad?"

"Up in his bedroom," says Rupert. "Shall I bash my new improved gong again and shout 'Breakfast is served'?" It's obvious he's itching to do it.

"Don't you dare!" My head's still humming from last time.

"This house is full of lazy people," Rupert lectures me in his smuggest voice. They should join The Early Rising Society! I've been up for ages doing really important stuff."

I don't want to know what he's been doing. Not before breakfast. Not if it's got anything to do with carrier bags and shovels and creeping behind dogs in the park. I slump at the kitchen table. "Where's the cornflakes?" I growl at no one in particular.

"We shall bring your breakfast to the table, madam," says Rupert, in a grovelly, Victorian servant's voice.

"Are you winding me up? I'm not in the mood," I warn him.

Ryan pops up from nowhere. "It's all fixed," he says.

"What is?" Instantly I'm on red alert. "Is this one of your inventions?" I say looking round. I can't see anything. Then I notice a little track. How did I miss it? I'm practically leaning my elbows on it. It's running in a circle round the kitchen table.

"I told you I was going to make a railway," says Ryan.

"I thought you meant a full-size one!"

"That would have been impossible, Rae," says Ryan, as if I've said something really silly. Then he gets talkative. It's the only time he does – when he's telling you about his inventions.

"No, this is an exact copy of a Victorian invention. They were mad about railways. They even invented this miniature one to serve the food up at banquets. It went chugging round the table, see, and people just helped themselves as it went past."

"Really?" Despite myself I'm impressed. I like that idea. At last there's something from the Victorian Age that sounds like good fun. "They should serve up our school dinners like that." I can just see it now. It would be great. We could put all our lunch tables in a big circle. And a cute little steam engine would puff round and round. And kids could just reach out as it went past their plates. And help themselves to food off the trucks. To pizza and chips and fishy penguins and yoghurts. And if you wanted more chips you could just wait until it chugged round again—

"But," says Rupert, breaking into my daydream, "we've got to have authentic Victorian food."

"So what's that then?"

"Jelly," he says, in a totally confident voice, as if there's no question about it. "The Victorians were jelly fiends. They were mad for it! They even made it in the shape of swans and castles—"

"And," interrupts Ryan, "I've just made a few minor improvements."

"To the jelly?" I ask him. I'm totally confused now. I've been confused ever since I woke up.

"To the train, of course," Ryan says impatiently, as if he's dealing with an idiot.

Before I can even say, "But I don't want jelly for breakfast!" they both spring into action.

Ryan slaps an engine down on the tracks. Wait a minute, it's not a sweet little chuffing steam engine, like I thought it would be, one that goes about the same speed as a snail. It's a sinister-looking black train with a nose as sharp as a shark's fin. Ryan hitches a flat truck to the back of it.

"Course, at a real banquet," says Rupert helpfully, "it would be a really long train with loads of trucks."

"You know those brilliant bullet trains in Japan," says Ryan, excitedly. "The ones that go at two hundred and seventy kilometres an hour—"

Big alarm bells are ringing in my brain. "That's not Victorian!"

"I know. But the Victorians would have had them, if they'd had the technology," he says, fiddling with some kind of remote control.

"My pudding," declares Rupert proudly, showing me a plate. Slopping about on it is the tallest, wobbliest, greenest jelly I've ever seen.

"It's supposed to be in the shape of a castle," says Rupert, as he slides the jelly on to the truck. "But I don't think it's quite set."

"Here she goes!" says Ryan.

The bullet train accelerates like a dragster – *zoom!* As Ryan's fingers dance over the controls, it speeds up even faster.

Whoosh – the jelly goes at warp speed. Once, twice, three times round and I still haven't managed to get my spoon in.

"Slow it down!" I scream.

The bullet train's making me dizzy, whizzing round and round the kitchen table with the jelly joggling about behind it. Now the train's just a black blur. The jelly's shaking about all over the place. Surely it can't stay in one piece. *Slurp!* A lump of green gunge flies off and just misses my nose. The jelly's being whirled to bits!

"Duck!" I shriek, flinging myself under the table and pulling Rupert with me.

Jelly's flying off in all directions. It's a jelly attack! It spatters the walls and windows then slides down like snot. *Splat, splat, splat.* It sprays the ceiling like a slime gun.

"Look at the mess. Stop it! Stop it! Mum'll go mad!"

"I can't. The train's out of control!" Ryan yells back. He chucks away the remote control, then dives to join us under the table. We peek out at the jelly storm raging all around us.

"It's got to stop soon!" Where's it all coming from? How can there be that much jelly in a jelly?

Kerrunch!

Something black just shot off the table and smashed at top speed into the kitchen wall.

"What was that!"

"My bullet train," says Ryan, sadly. "It was going too fast to take the bend."

It's lying there, ruined, in a whirring heap. There's no jelly left on the truck. It's spread all round the room instead.

We stagger out from under the table.

"Maybe," I tell Ryan, "it's not such a good idea to serve school dinners by train." Especially not custard or mashed potato.

"Oh, dear," says Rupert. "Mum's not going to like this."

"You're not kidding," says someone from the doorway.

It's Dad. "What on earth's going on?" he says, staring round at the jelly-blasted walls and the smoking wreck of Ryan's train.

"One of Ryan's inventions," I tell him, shrugging.

"Oh, right," Dad sighs, as if that explains everything.

Dad's wearing a top hat. It's really tall and black. And that fuzzy caterpillar isn't on his top lip any more. There's a small brown furry animal there instead.

"Dad! You're wearing a false moustache!" says Rupert.

"I know," says Dad. "It was in that parcel. Is this macho or what? Look how it curls at the ends! And your mum was right. It goes a treat with this top hat."

Rupert opens his mouth to say something rude. I give him a threatening glare. We're in enough trouble already.

"Course, I shouldn't be wearing it really," says Dad, looking a bit guilty. "Top hats are far too posh for Rent-a-Rabble. I'm just trying to get the *total* Victorian experience."

I don't think that's the reason. I think he's wearing it because Mum fancies him in it.

"Don't worry, Rae," says Dad, seeing me looking doubtful. "I won't be wearing this for our Victorian job. I'm going to be someone much more common."

"So have you decided who you're going to be, Dad?" asks Rupert, trying not to snigger. That moustache is really over the top. How can it be big and bushy and curly at the same time?

"I've got some ideas. But that's what I wanted to talk to you about. We ought to have a big brainstorming session and settle what we're all going to be. I mean, time's getting on. We've only got until Sunday."

"Let's do it now," shouts Rupert, eagerly. "Let's have an important breakfast meeting like Mum does."

"What, in this kitchen?" I say, looking round at the mess.

Dad frowns. "Rae's right. We can't even have breakfast in here until it's cleaned up." He thinks a bit, then he says, "Tell you what, kids. We'll tackle this later. Let's go and have our family meeting in the supermarket café. They do an excellent all-day-breakfast there."

"Brilliant idea, Dad," says Rupert.

"But no feeling babies' heads this time," warns Dad.

"*On, ris!*" says Rupert, saluting.

Chapter Five

Dad drives us in our beat-up old van to the café.

Everyone we pass stares at Rent-a-Rabble's slogans: *Need a scullion, a serf or an underling? Then pick up that phone and give us a ring!*

They're scratching their heads and looking puzzled. You can practically hear them saying, "*Doh!* What's going on?"

I don't blame them. I spend a lot of time, when I'm working for Rent-a Rabble, asking myself the same question.

A man in a white van honks at Dad for going too slowly. "Just tell him to get lost," says Rupert, making rude faces out of the window. "Tell him you're going at an authentic Victorian speed!"

"Rupert!" says Dad, sounding rattled. "Don't do that! That man looks the violent type. He's shaking his fist!"

Because Dad's telling him off, Rupert turns down his mouth like a tragic clown.

"You look like all those misery-guts in Victorian photos," I laugh at him.

Ryan says, out of the blue, "All Victorians look miserable in photos. It took ages to take a photo in the early days of photography. Sometimes twenty minutes. You try smiling for that long."

"I could do it!" says Rupert, suddenly curving his mouth up into a banana shape. "I could smile for longer than that! "*Kool. Mi gnilims!*" His face cracks up into a big, beaming smile.

"Look what you've done now," I whisper to Ryan.

But my big brother's got a brain like a kangaroo. It's already hopping ahead to another idea.

"In Victorian times," he tells Dad, "that top hat would make you a target for garrotters."

"Garrotters?" I ask Ryan. You can see Rupert's dying to ask questions as well. But he can't. He's too busy trying for some kind of smiling record.

"Yep," says Ryan. "In Victorian times everyone was scared of garrotters. One guy would sneak up behind you and try to strangle you with his scarf. And while you were struggling his mate would pick your pockets."

"And Ryan's right about the top hat," says Dad. "One look at this and those garrotters would think, 'He's got loads of dosh! Let's get him!'"

I forgot to say. Dad's still got his top hat and false moustache on. No, I'm not cringing with embarrassment. Not much, anyway. Dad's always going out in public in historical costume. He doesn't mind the stares. He's on a mission. He thinks we should all make history a big part of our daily lives. Besides, if I see any of my friends I can always pretend he's a complete stranger.

I sneak another look at Rupert. What's wrong with him? He's like a shark. His face is fixed in a terrible toothy grin.

"That's why I've brought along this little invention –" Ryan's saying. For the first time I notice he's got his backpack. What's in there? I bet it's something really hi-tech. It's making a strange humming sound, like a computer.

"Show me later, Ryan," says Dad. He's looking for a parking space. He finds one next to the kiddies' adventure playground.

Rupert shoves past me to get out. That smile is getting worse. It looks really scary now. Like a mad axe-murderer in a horror film.

"Will you stop smiling like that? It's giving me the creeps!"

Rupert silently shakes his head. You've got to be impressed. My little bro's so stubborn. When he decides to do something he never, ever gives up.

I jump out after him. Where's he going in such a hurry?

Then I see what he's up to. "Dad! Come quick! It's Rupert!"

Dad comes rushing round the side of the van. Rupert's smiling that awful maniac's smile. He's creeping in a sinister way up to the playground. He's just spotted an innocent baby on the grass. It's lying beside its mum on a blanket, kicking its chubby little legs and gurgling. And its white baldy head is glittering in the sun.

"Rupert! NO!" me and Dad yell, both at once.

But Rupert's tiptoeing closer. He's grinning like a ghoul. His arms are stretched out. His fingers are twitching. He's just about to give the baby's bonce a quick feel.

Then the baby spots him. It sees that axe-murderer's smile.

It opens its mouth into a big square shape, "Waaaaaa!"

I start running. I rugby tackle Rupert just as he's going in for a second try.

"What do you think you're doing?" yells a shocked mum. "How dare you frighten my baby?"

Rupert can't answer. He just smiles at her, like a wolf who hasn't eaten dinner for days.

"Sorry, sorry," I grovel, as I drag Rupert away. "He's a bit strange."

Dad catches up. Between us we haul Rupert back to the van. Halfway there Rupert checks his watch. Then his face starts jerking about and twitching horribly. He seems to be trying to alter it. But he can't shift that smile.

"It's stuck!" he cries in a strangled voice. "Now I've got to smile for the rest of my life!"

Then his face suddenly rearranges itself so it looks almost normal. "Only kidding!" he says.

"See, I did it, Rae!" he shouts triumphantly. "Smiling for twenty minutes is possible. Those Victorians should have tried a bit harder when they had their picture taken."

Dad tries one of his weedy telling-offs. "Rupert, you've got to stop sneaking up on babies. It's becoming a habit."

Then I take over. "You complete and utter idiot!" I snarl at Rupert. "Don't you ever learn? Never, *ever* feel the baldy heads of people's babies. They don't like it. And they don't like it even more when you tell them their kid is a criminal!"

Rupert opens his mouth. Is he going to make a cheeky remark in backwards language, like "*Maebnus*" for instance? But he doesn't dare. He can see I'm hopping mad.

Ryan comes drifting up. "Where were you when we needed you?" I ask him.

"Why?" he says, looking vaguely round. "What's happened?"

Dad takes a deep breath. "I think I'm ready for that breakfast now," he says, heading towards the supermarket.

Chapter Six

In the supermarket, Dad looks around nervously. "I hope there are none of those mums here from yesterday."

"Remember, keep away from babies!" he warns Rupert.

But Rupert's got a butterfly brain. He's forgotten about feeling bald bonces. He's got other things on his mind.

"Look at all these ladies showing their ankles!" he says, sounding shocked. "They should disguise them! They should put frills round them."

"For heaven's sake, Rupert!" hisses Dad, hustling him into the café.

"Victorians thought ankles were rude. I'm only being authentic," protests Rupert. That's always his excuse when he shows us up in public. Personally, I think he just loves being a pain in the neck.

In the café, people can't help staring. It's not every day you see someone queuing for food in a top hat and big curly false moustache. But Dad doesn't even notice. He's probably forgotten he's got them on.

"Right," says Dad, after we've found a table for our breakfast meeting. "Time to get focused, people. We've got to choose our Victorian characters."

He stabs at his sausage and takes a bite.

"Picture this, kids," he says, his eyes shining with enthusiasm. He waves his fork around, with the sausage on the end. "A typical Victorian street scene, where rich and poor mingle. There are shops – a draper's, a druggist, a hatter's, a pawnbroker's. There are street traders. The poor, ragged, shoeless girl selling watercress. The pie man crying, 'Buy my fine pies!' It's chaos! There's a traffic jam of carriages and carts! And in-between skips the pickpocket—"

"Can I be a pickpocket, Dad?" cries Rupert. "Look, I've got a lady's hands."

A man at the next table checks his wallet hasn't been lifted. But Dad doesn't even hear. He's inspired.

"There are posh town houses, yes," cries Dad, "but close by are stinking slums and reeking rivers! Rivers full of blood and guts from slaughterhouses, dye from factories, dead rats and floating dung –"

The lady at the table next to us pushes away her chocolate eclair.

"– and terrible diseases—" Dad starts up again.

"Dad," interrupts Rupert, who hasn't been the centre of attention for two minutes. "Look what I've collected." He shows Dad a supermarket carrier bag. Tied with string. I didn't even see him bring it in.

"No!" I hiss, horrified. I'm used to Rupert

being disgusting. But this is going too far. "You can't open that in here!"

He does. "It's my brush collection, Dad." He turns to me. His eyes are all wide and innocent. "Why, what did you think it was, Rae? I've decided, Dad. Those Victorian streets were one big horse toilet. So I'm definitely going to be a crossing sweeper. I don't want to be a poor little chimney sweep. Don't send me up chimneys, Dad," begs Rupert in his loud, booming voice.

"*Shhh, shhh!*" soothes Dad, looking round anxiously. "Who said anything about sending you up chimneys? A crossing sweeper is an excellent choice. I'm proud, son. You couldn't have picked anyone more humble."

"And smelly," adds Rupert.

"These brushes are no good," says Dad, glancing into Rupert's carrier bag. "You need a long-handled one for sweeping up horse dung. I'll tell you what son, I'll buy you a brand new one. They sell them in here. You can choose your very own broom."

"My very own broom!" Rupert clasps his hands together in delight. He seems thrilled.

"Thanks, Dad!" Surely he's putting it on? He sees me rolling my eyes.

"I'm being authentic, Rae!" he says. "A crossing sweeper's broom was his most precious possession, wasn't it, Dad?"

He looks at Dad for approval.

"Creep," I hiss at him.

"And Rebel's going to be my faithful hound," declares Rupert.

A crossing sweeper's dog? I can't imagine Rebel will be over the moon about that. "Well, I'm not going to tell him," I warn Rupert.

Then Dad says, "And we already know what you're going to be, Rae."

"Do we?" This is the first I've heard about it. "I thought I could choose."

"But I got an e-mail from the organizers this morning," explains Dad. "They want one of us to be a slavey. And since a slavey's a girl, it's got to be you. Luckily, there's a slavey's costume in that parcel—"

"A *slavey*?" I interrupt him. "That sounds really humble."

"It is!" says Dad, as if I've been really lucky. "A slavey is a maidservant who does all the roughest work. Scrubbing the floor, humping buckets of coal upstairs—"

"I wanted to be a Used Tea Leaf Seller."

"But you'll be in the big house," says Dad. "It'll be a typical Victorian scene. The servants slaving away downstairs, the rich people having a good time upstairs—"

"Wait a minute," I interrupt him again. "Who's playing these rich people having a good time while I'm working my butt off?"

"Well," says Dad uneasily. "You know that boy Nigel out of your class, and his mum?"

Oh, no. He must be joking. Not that weaselly creep Nigel and his snooty mum.

"Yes," explains Dad. "Nigel's mum will be mistress of the house. And Nigel will be the young master."

"Can I be the young master, Dad?" shouts Rupert, just because he hasn't said anything for five seconds.

Ryan suddenly speaks, which surprises everyone. Sometimes you forget he's there at all.

"Did you know," he says in that dreamy way of his, "that in Victorian times, boys wore girls' frocks until they were five or six years old?"

Rupert instantly changes his mind. "Oh, no, Dad. I don't want to be a young master. Don't make me wear girls' clothes!" he pleads in his foghorn voice. "Please don't make me, Dad! Don't make me!"

People are staring. They're looking shocked. Dad grits his teeth and hisses, "For heaven's sake, Rupert, shut up!"

I've decided. I just can't stand those two giving me orders.

"No!" I tell Dad, desperately. "No way! Not for a million pounds. I'm not going to be a slavey!"

"But it'll be really exciting!" says Dad. "Because there's something I didn't realize about this job. That's the other thing that e-mail told me. Kids, it's all going to be on the internet!"

"The net!" says Rupert. "Wow!"

"Yes," says Dad. "There'll be hidden cameras and microphones set up every-where in the Victorian street, and in the big house. They're filming the whole thing live! People will be able to log on and see and hear Victorian life as it happens. Isn't that great?"

Is he trying to get me to feel better about being a slavey? He's just making things worse. Being live on the net means all my friends will be able to *watch* me being bossed about by Nigel and his mum.

I've suddenly thought of something really important. "What's Raymond going to be?" I ask Dad.

Raymond is Nigel's minder. He hasn't got any brains. But that doesn't bother him because he's built like the Incredible Hulk. Wherever Nigel goes, Raymond goes. And they've both got a big grudge against Rent-a-Rabble because of what happened on our Elizabethan job.

"Who's Raymond?" says Dad, vaguely. "Anyhow, there's another thing I need to tell you. There's a prize for the Most Convincing Victorian Character. It's two hundred pounds! Of course, you have to be *strictly* Victorian all day and not do or say anything modern. And remember, you could be spied on at any time. It's not as easy as it seems—"

"So what's my costume like?" I interrupt Dad.

My dad's scatter-brained but he's not stupid. He knows why I'm asking about the costume.

"Oh," says Dad, casually, "there's a long dress and a great big pinny you wrap around you. And a big, frilly mob cap that hides your hair and face almost completely. And the bit of face you *could* see would be grimy from all that grease and coal dust. Even your own friends wouldn't know you."

Dad knows he's got me interested. I'd really like to win that prize. I'm already making plans in my head for how I'll spend the money.

"Can I have shoes this time, Dad?" I ask him.

"Yes!" says Dad, as if it's a big thrill. "You get to wear button-up boots."

"So what are you going to be, Dad?" asks Rupert.

No one bothers to ask Ryan. He does the same thing at all our Rent-a-Rabble jobs. Drifts around in brown rags and bare feet being a peasant. And causes chaos with his inventions. He's bought that humming bag in from the van. I've just noticed. What's it supposed to do? Stop you being garrotted? But why does he need it in here?

Please *leave the invention in the bag, Ryan,* I'm thinking. The people in the café already think we're the family from hell. And that Dad is a cruel monster who sends Rupert up chimneys wearing girls' frocks.

"What am I going to be?" says Dad, finally answering Rupert's question. "It's a tough one. In Victorian times, there are so many hungry, homeless down-and-outs to choose from. I might be a poor, penniless soul who ends up in the workhouse or—"

"Why don't you be a pig man, Dad?" interrupts Rupert.

"Pardon?"

"You know, a humble pig man who comes in from the country to sell his *one and only* pig in town?"

I can see what's coming. Rupert's got that sneaky look on his face. Why can't Dad see it too?

But Dad isn't suspicious like me. He falls

for it. "You know, that's a good idea, son," he says. "A simple country yokel who's completely confused by the modern world. That part would suit me down to the ground!"

I say, sarcastically, "And just who's going to play this one and only pig? As if we didn't know!"

Honestly, Rupert can twist Dad round his little finger. He says, as if he's only just thought of it, "What about Gilbert, Dad?"

Gilbert is this historical pig who gets hired out for events, just like us. On our last two jobs, Rupert and Gilbert were best friends.

"Do we have to have him, Dad?" I object immediately. "He stinks!"

"Don't say rude things about my mate!" says Rupert. "Me and that pig are like that." He crosses two fingers and shakes them in my face.

And Dad says, in his most serious voice. "There's nothing wrong with stinking, Rae. The poor folk Rent-a-Rabble play couldn't keep themselves clean, no matter how hard they tried. They had no soap or water supply—"

"Yes, yes, Dad, spare me the lecture! I know they couldn't help being smelly."

Then Ryan says, right out of the blue. "Want to try my invention, Dad?"

Straight away, there's a struggle going on on Dad's face. He wants to encourage Ryan. But at the same time, it gets him really upset when Ryan improves on history.

"What is it?" ask Dad warily. Ryan's answer confirms Dad's worst fears.

"It's a new improved top hat," says Ryan, "for getting rid of garrotters."

He lifts the home-made top hat out of his bag. It's tall and black like Dad's other one. But it's made out of some kind of rubbery stuff. What is that weird humming? Has the hat got a motor inside?

From being almost totally silent Ryan suddenly gets really talkative.

"Picture this, Dad! Those evil garrotters are sneaking up behind you, right! But you've no need to worry, long as you've got my anti-garrotting hat on. Go on, give it a go."

"Dad," I warn him. "Are you *sure* this is a good idea?"

"What harm can a top hat do?" laughs Dad.

He takes off his ordinary top hat. Then puts Ryan's invention on. He bashes the hat down firmly on his head. "It's a much snugger fit than the other one," he says. That humming gets louder – and angrier.

"I've got this buzzing noise in my ears. . ." complains Dad.

Ryan gets up out of his seat. He creeps round the table.

"Right. I am a Victorian garrotter, Dad. I'm going to strangle you. While your pockets are being picked by my pickpocketing partner."

"That must be me!" says Rupert leaping up joyfully. If he tells the whole café that he's got a lady's hands again, I'm going to kill him.

"It works better if you stand up, Dad," says Ryan.

Dad looks puzzled. He pushes his chair back. "What, like this?" In a flash, Ryan whips out a long blue scarf and flings it over Dad's head.

"*Urggh!*" Dad's head is forced back. He grabs at his throat. The whole café is staring!

"*Urgle urgle!*" Dad's making horrible choking sounds.

Rupert pounces and starts picking Dad's pockets. "Hey, I'm dead good at this!" His flickering fingers are fast as lightning.

"Ryan, Ryan, that scarf is too tight!" I yell. Everyone in the café has stopped eating. They look seriously worried. "Call Security!" says someone.

"Ryan, you're strangling him!"

"That's what I'm supposed to be doing," puffs Ryan. "But it's all right, Dad. You can save yourself. All you've got to do is pull this little lever. It's here, Dad, on your hat."

Dad's face is getting redder and redder: "*Nurrgh!*" But he must have heard because he forces his hand up to the hat and pulls. . .

The top of the hat flips open. *Buzzzzz!* A swarm of wasps comes zooming out. They're really mad. They must have been trapped in there for hours.

"Ryan, what's going on?" I've heard of bees in your bonnet. But wasps in your top hat?

"It works!" Ryan loosens his grip on Dad's neck. "See, Dad. You've scared me off. I'm running away –" He takes big, slow-motion steps to the other side of the café.

"*Urgh!*" Dad staggers about trying to get his breath back. "Ryan!" he gasps. "Did you have to be so realistic?"

"We are Rent-a-Rabble, the *real* history people," Ryan reminds him.

Buzz! Dad bats the air wildly with his hands. "*Ow! Ow!* I think I've been stung!" He tugs the top hat off his head and hurls it away.

"Gerroff! Gerroff!" Rupert screams at the wasps. He dives under a table.

The whole café is panicking. "Run! Run!" People's arms are whirling like windmills. The wasps are dive-bombing chocolate eclairs, getting stuck to iced buns, drowning in lemonade –

"There's one in my hair. Get it out! Get it out!"

A frantic lady whops the air with her handbag. She rushes for the exit. The wasps stream after her: *Buzzzzzz!* It must be her flowery perfume.

The sound of trampling feet dies away. It's very peaceful now in the café.

Rupert crawls out from under the table. "Have the wasps gone?"

"Everyone's gone," I tell him, looking round at the toppled tables and overturned chairs.

"I'll have this cheeseburger then," Rupert says, nicking it off a nearby table. "If it's going to waste –"

"*Er*, Ryan," says Dad, apologetically. "I don't want to crush your enthusiasm or anything. But I think that invention of yours was a bit of a disaster." These are tough words for Dad. But Ryan doesn't sound devastated.

"You're right, Dad," he says cheerfully, as if he hasn't just emptied an entire café in ten seconds. "It was far too low-tech. It was effective. *But not effective enough.*"

He picks the hat up off the floor. It's a bit battered. He stuffs it in his backpack. Then drifts out of the café. He's already planning the Anti-Garrotting Top Hat, Mark II.

It's spookily silent in the supermarket. There's hardly anyone around. Ryan's already gone back to the van. But Dad and Rupert and me walk down the empty aisles to the Household Goods section.

"Dad," I say, nervously. "Don't you think we ought to get out of here?" How far can wasps chase people? Those shoppers will be back any second. And they're not going to be in a good mood.

"He promised!" says Rupert, his bottom lip sliding out like a fat, pink slug.

"All right, son, all right," soothes Dad. "You shall have your new broom!"

How come Rupert always gets what he wants? You wouldn't think he'd just tried to pick his own dad's pockets.

Rupert leaps forwards. He grabs one of the brooms. "Cool! This is the one I want, Dad. This is a perfect crossing sweeper's broom!"

He carries it proudly to the checkouts. "My lovely broom," he murmurs to it, cuddling the bristly bit to his cheek. "I shall look after you always."

I shake my head sadly. Being best friends with a pig was bad enough. But now he thinks hugging a broom is cool. Doesn't he care what other kids think of him?

People are crowding back into the café. I breathe a sigh of relief when nobody seems to blame us. Maybe they weren't sure where those wasps came from. Rent-a-Rabble is off the hook again.

Dad feels his face, then looks glum. "I've lost my Victorian false moustache, Rae," he says. "And Mum really fancied me in it. It must be back there in the café."

He's about to suggest going back to look for it. But just as he opens his mouth, a scream comes from the café. "*Eek!* There's a dead weasel in my all-day-breakfast!"

"Sorry, Dad," I tell him, taking him gently by the arm and leading him out to the van. "I think you'd better forget about that false moustache. Besides, we need to get busy. We've got a kitchen to clean before Mum comes home."

Chapter Seven

BONG!!!!

The whole house seems to be shaking. My eardrums are buzzing like wasps. Wasps? No, I'd rather not think about them.

Bong!

"Breakfast is served!" It's Rupert with his stereo gong. Wait till I catch him, waking me up like that. What time is it?

Sleepily, I stretch a hand out from under my duvet and fumble around on my bedside table for my Bart Simpson alarm clock. It's only six a.m! I forgot, Rupert is a member of The Early Rising Society.

"If he comes in here and tries to fine me, he's dead."

It's the day before Victorian Day and Rent-a-Rabble has got loads to do. I tried my slavey's costume on last night. Dad's right. It's a great disguise. With that big, floppy mob cap on and my face all dirty, no one will ever guess it's me, Rae Rabble.

It's going to be tough winning that two hundred pounds. I mean, without doing something drastic to Nigel and his mum. I've done some reading about slaveys in big houses. They get bossed about by everyone. They light fires, scrub steps, lug buckets of coal and hot water upstairs, dust rooms, beat carpets. It's backbreaking! And the mistress of the house just sits around on her bustle all day.

But I'm going to have to bite my tongue and play it humble. We're on CCTV all the time. And slaveys aren't supposed to talk back.

"You can do it, Rae!" I tell myself. "Just a bit of suffering. And then you can get your own back on Nigel later." As long as Raymond, his muscle-man minder, isn't around.

Still only half-awake, I go stumbling into the bathroom.

"Rupert!" I scream. "Get up here. NOW!"

The toilet isn't frilly any more. You don't have to hunt for the seat. Instead, there's a big sign on it, written in red crayon, that says, "THIS IS NOT A TOILET."

"You called?" Rupert skids into the bathroom. He's clutching his new crossing sweeper's broom. He goes wild if you try to take it away from him. I bet he even took it to bed with him last night. I'm going to have to write to my magazine about him. *Dear Problem Page, my brother's in love with a broom.*

"What's all this about, then?" I ask him, jabbing my thumb at the sign.

"Oh," he says. "Mum made me take off the frills. So I put up that sign. It's psychology. Mind over matter, right? If an easily shocked Victorian lady comes in, she can sit there and think, *This is NOT A toilet. This is NOT a toilet!* And then she won't get embarrassed. Right?"

I sigh. "Rupert," I tell him. "You're really weird. Do you know that?" I slump into a kitchen chair. "Has Mum gone to work yet?"

"No," says Rupert. "She's around here somewhere."

"Where's Ryan, then?"

"He's out in the garage. He's inventing like crazy!"

Oh, dear, I wish Rupert hadn't told me that. "He's not taking any of his inventions to the museum tomorrow, is he?"

Mum comes in. She's already dressed in her business suit. She takes a quick look at her watch. "Just time for a cup of coffee," she says, "before I dash off."

"Are you coming to Victorian Day tomorrow, Mum?" I ask her. She did come once, to our Elizabethan job. That's when Dad's inflated calves went down, making very rude raspberry noises. Victorian ladies would have fainted with the shock.

"*Er*, no," says Mum, rather too quickly. "Of course, I'd love to come. But my day tomorrow is packed with business meetings. Work, work, work!" she says, looking relieved. Mum quite often works at the weekend.

Rupert comes in. Someone is going to have to tell him that carrying a broom everywhere you go isn't cool.

He's up to something. He's got that crafty gleam in his eyes.

"Mum," he says, "you could get some free advertising for your firm tomorrow."

"Oh, yes?" Mum answers. She doesn't look all that interested. "This Victorian thing you're doing is going out on the net, isn't it?"

"Yeah," says Rupert, sounding sneaky. "Loads of people will log on. And whenever they do, the name of Cropper and Crouch could hit them right in the eye!"

To my amazement, Mum seems to be thinking about it. "Actually," she says, "it would be quite appropriate. My firm was founded in Victorian times. Cropper and Crouch is highly respected. With lots of very important clients. So this advertising you're talking about would have to be tasteful."

"Oh, it will be!" Rupert promises. He rushes out with his broom before Mum can ask him any more questions.

"I've just remembered, Rae," says Mum. "We've got one of those lovely old enamel signs at work, with the name of our firm on it. It would look just right in a Victorian street scene."

I've got enough on my mind without thinking about old signs. But I can see Mum's quite excited about it. "It's about time my firm got its name on the net," she says. "And this way we won't have to pay a penny."

"Or even a farthing." Don't know why I said that. It's a feeble joke. And my mum never jokes about money. But it is only six-thirty in the morning.

Rupert rushes back in. "I've just thought," he says. "I think you should pay Rent-a-Rabble some money."

I can read Rupert's crafty little mind. If Rent-a-Rabble earn a bit extra for this Victorian job, Dad might pay us a bonus. Rupert's got his dreams too. I can guess what they are – he wants to raise enough cash to buy Gilbert, his piggy chum.

Mum frowns. "How much?" she asks, suspiciously.

"Fifty pounds?" suggests Rupert, just grabbing a number out of the air. He's amazed when Mum agrees. She gets out her calculator first and does some quick sums.

"Cheap at the price," she says.

"A hundred pounds! A thousand pounds!" shouts Rupert wildly.

"Don't push your luck, sunshine," says Mum, gulping down the last of her coffee. "I'll bring that sign home from work tonight. OK?"

She dashes out the door. Dad comes into the kitchen. "Oh, dear," he says. "Has Mum gone? I wanted to model my pig man costume. What do you think, kids."

"You're wearing a frock!" says Rupert, shocked. "It looks sissy!"

"It's a *smock*, Rupert," Dad corrects him, fussily. "Lots of humble farm labourers wore them. *They* didn't think they looked sissy. And they were big, tough, muscly men!"

"Does it have to be so, well, *flared out*?" I ask him, trying to be tactful.

"It's very authentic," says Dad, sounding hurt. "Look at this lovely criss-cross embroidery on the front."

Me and Rupert exchange glances. I'm really glad that slavey costume is going to be such a good disguise.

"Yes, I shall wear my smock with pride!" declares Dad. Oh, no, here he goes again. "Because it is the garment of the poor, oppressed peasant. Just like my great-grandad who used to dig turnips from dawn to dusk for tuppence a day—"

"Did you get Gilbert?" demands Rupert suddenly. My little bro's busy brain has skipped to something else. Something that matters to him a lot more than Dad looking like a twig wearing a tepee.

"*Er*, yes," says Dad, annoyed at being interrupted just as he was getting warmed up. "It wasn't easy. He's a very popular pig. But his owner says he's got a space in his diary."

Rupert looks ecstatic. "I'm gonna be meeting my best friend again!" He would have clasped his hands together. Only he can't because he's clutching his broom.

Sometimes, I worry about Rupert. Is he right in the head? How's he going to look after himself in the big, wide world? Or are other little brothers as strange as he is?

Ryan drifts in to get himself a drink. He's taking a quick break from inventing.

"*Er*, Ryan," says Dad, nervously. "What kind of gizmos are you actually planning to take tomorrow? I hope they're all strictly authentic. Remember Rent-a-Rabble's motto: *We Tell It Like It Was!*"

Ryan says, "Well, I was going to invent something for Rupert that's more efficient than that broom. A sort of massively powerful street hoover to suck up horse dung." Dad looks a bit alarmed.

But Rupert goes bananas. He clutches his trusty broom even tighter. "I don't want any evil, new-fangled machinery. I just want my broom."

"It would have been really useful in the park," Ryan tries to coax him, "you know, when you were being that Victorian dog-dirt collector—"

"Don't encourage him to start that again!" I warn Ryan.

"I – JUST – WANT – MY – LITTLE – BROOM!" Rupert roars.

Dad sighs. "Don't get upset, Rupert. In any case, there won't *actually* be any horse dung. There isn't room for real horses in the Victorian Street. So you'll only be *pretending* to sweep it up, right?"

To my surprise, Rupert isn't disappointed. "Good!" he says. "I'm glad it's only pretend horse dung. I don't want to get my lovely new brush all dirty, do I?"

"Anyway, I did the drawing for this super-powerful street hoover," says Ryan. "But I didn't have time to make it. Because I'm working on my new improved Anti-Garrotting Top Hat."

"A good idea, son," says Dad, looking relieved about the hoover. "As long as this hat hasn't got any wasps in it! But I shan't be able to wear it, of course," he adds, sounding a bit too pleased. "A top hat isn't at all right for this pig man's costume."

He picks up a letter from the table. It says URGENT on it in big red letters. It's from the bank. But Dad's already folding it into a little square tray with sides. He puts the tray on his head.

"The very poorest people in Victorian times wore paper hats," Dad tells us.

"Dad," I say, "are you making this up?"

"No!" Dad looks hurt. "I wouldn't do that. It's an absolutely authentic detail. And remember what we say at Rent-a-Rabble: *The Drama's in the Detail!*"

Dad wanders off in his smock with his paper hat on his head. Don't ask me to say anything. Just feel sorry for me. Right?

"I don't want a super-hoover!" howls Rupert.

"For heaven's sake, Rupert," I tell him. "Stop going over the top. He told you. He hasn't made it yet."

But Rupert never misses a chance to make a big scene. "It sounds dead dangerous! I might get sucked up in it. I might end up in hospital! And then I'd have to wear Queen Victoria's underwear."

Even Ryan goes goggle-eyed. "What do you mean – Queen Victoria's underwear?"

"She donated her old underwear to hospitals!" wails Rupert. "Like her bloomers and

76

stuff. And poor people had to wear them and look grateful! 'Cos she was the QUEEN. I bet that underwear's still around! I bet there's poor people in hospitals being *forced* to wear her cheesy old bloomers even TODAY!"

"Look what you've done," I tell Ryan. "You've really upset him now! Just forget about that hoover. In fact, forget about taking *any* of your inventions along tomorrow!"

But there's about as much chance of that as there is of Rent-a-Rabble managing to do a job without messing it up.

Chapter Eight

It's the big day at last. We've all got our costumes on and we're loaded into the Rent-a-Rabble van ready to go to the City Museum.

Rebel's decided to come along. He wasn't crazy about being a crossing sweeper's dog, but Rupert persuaded him. "There might be some lady dogs there you can chat up," he told him.

Dad gives us our last instructions. "Don't forget, kids! There's a cash prize for Most Convincing Victorian Character. So watch your tongue, Rae. Slaveys do what they're told and never, ever talk back."

This is going to be torture. Nigel is the sworn foe of us Rabbles – I just know he's going to get right up my nose. But Nigel's snooty mum as my mistress? Give me a break!

And what about Raymond, the man-mountain? He's bound to be there. Nigel hardly goes anywhere without him.

There are only two things that stop me from backing out of this job right now. One, I don't want to let Dad down; and two, I desperately need the money.

"How come Nigel's mum isn't Queen Victoria?" I mutter to Dad. *She'd* never be proud to play a peasant. She always has to be a VIP.

Then Ryan asks, "Are the public allowed into the Victorian Street today?"

Why's he want to know that? He's not planning to involve the public in his inventions again, is he? Even though I told him not to, he's brought along his new improved Anti-Garrotting Top Hat. But, I mean, how much damage can you do with a *hat*?

"No," says Dad, shocked at the suggestion. "Letting the public in would ruin the atmosphere. Can you imagine it? Someone in jeans and a T-shirt, maybe eating a McDonald's or talking on their mobile, strolling right into camera-shot?"

Good. No public. Rent-a-Rabble and the public don't get on. There was nearly a riot at our medieval job.

"But history fans can log on at home," says Dad excitedly. "It's the new way of visiting museums – without moving from your chair."

Good again. I can't imagine my mates will be rushing to log on. And even if they do, they won't know me. I've got that mob cap pulled down to my eyebrows. And the rest of my face is smeared with grease and dirt.

With any luck this Victorian Day will slip by without anyone noticing I'm in it.

"Don't you think you've overdone the

camouflage, Rae?" says Dad. "You look like a commando going on a dangerous mission into enemy territory."

Strange, but that's exactly how I feel.

"OK, kids? Here we go!"

Dad starts up the van. He pulls out into the road. Dad's driving in his pig man's smock and home-made paper hat. But we don't even get one curious glance from our neighbours. They're used to living next to Rent-a-Rabble by now.

Rupert says, looking puzzled, "What have you given me this big sign for, Rae?"

"For heaven's sake. I told you! It's the sign for Mum's firm." Why is he being so dozy about it? He's the one who set up this advertising deal.

"Mum said make sure to stick it right in front of a camera," I remind him. "She'll be logging on to check she's getting her money's worth."

"But I don't need a sign," insists Rupert.

Is he being deliberately dense? "Then how are you going to advertise Mum's firm? You'd better make sure it's tasteful. She's got some very important clients."

He mutters something I can't hear. Then Dad says, "We've arrived!"

Rupert rushes out of the van with Rebel. Then he dashes back for his broom.

"I nearly forgot you, my lovely little broom!" he says, cuddling it.

He's talking to it now! It's sad, really. Then he picks up a paint can and brush. "I nearly forgot these as well," he says. "I was so excited about seeing Gilbert."

What's he want paint for? But I haven't got time to worry about that. Rebel will keep an eye on him. I've got problems of my own.

I go trudging into the museum. There's a whole Victorian street built inside, under a big glass dome. And it's brilliant, much better than I expected. It's really bustling and lively. There are shops to go into. And crowds of people in Victorian costumes all over the place.

There's a muffin man ringing his bell: "Get your fresh-baked muffins here!" And a guy playing a barrel organ, and a lavender lady calling, "Buy my fine lavender!"

"Hey, this is all right," I tell Ryan. He was right next to me, dressed in the raggy clothes of a street urchin. But he's gone off on his own private business.

A kid in a sailor suit runs past me, bowling a hoop over the cobbles.

This is really cheery! I'm thinking. I feel optimistic! Maybe, this time, nothing will go wrong.

Someone's saying, "Remember, people, the cameras go on at nine sharp. And from then on you're one hundred per cent Victorian until they go off again at five."

I can't see Raymond anywhere. Maybe I can forget about him. Maybe he's being menacing somewhere else.

Some lady ticks off my name on a list and shows me where the house is. It's between the barber's and the hatter's – a tall skinny house with four floors.

"You're down in the kitchen," she says. "That's right at the bottom of the house." That figures. Right at the bottom is where us Rabbles usually end up

I go hurrying in, down some steps from the street and into a little side door.

The kitchen's like a cave. It's cold and dark as a dungeon with big stone sinks and a massive black stove. There are loads of copper jelly moulds hanging on the walls. Rupert was right – those Victorians took jelly seriously.

The only thing that's not Victorian is the camera, stuck up there in the corner of the ceiling. Oh no, it's moving. It's looking my way. It must be nine o'clock already. I'd better start being obedient from NOW!

Brinnng!

A jangling bell makes me nearly jump out of my skin. What's all that about, then? Then I realize. It's the bell to call the servants. Somebody wants me upstairs.

Chapter Nine

I'm clattering up the stairs from the kitchen. My button-up boots are too clumpy. My long frock keeps tripping me up. How did slaveys work in these stupid clothes?

Now I'm puffing into the parlour. It's crammed with sofas and chairs and ornaments and little round tables and ferns in pots. You can hardly turn round in here!

I'm being watched and it's not by cameras. There are eyes goggling at me through the gloom. The hairs start prickling on the back of my neck. Then I realize, they're dead birds and animals. Eagles and owls and even baby hares. All stuffed and put in glass cases.

I'm just shuddering and saying to myself, "That's so spooky!" when someone cries, in a haughty voice, "Ah, the servant! About time too. I rang that bell a good ninety seconds ago."

It's Nigel's mum. I mistook her for an extra-large armchair. She's wearing a frock made out of some stiff black stuff. It's got a bustle the size of a wheelie bin. She comes crackling over like the Black Widow with all her jet-black jewellery jangling.

"And pray, what is your name, girl?"

"She's called Rabble," says another voice.

Someone gets up out of a chair. He's dressed in a tweedy jacket with matching tweedy knickerbockers. But I'd know that weaselly face anywhere. It's Nigel. And he saw right through my slavey disguise. Nigel's smarter than he looks.

"*Ahhh*, Raddle!" says Nigel's mum. "Fetch me more coal for the fire."

Who's she think she is? Giving me orders? She can't even get my name right! I nearly tell her, "Fetch it yourself!"

Be humble, Rae! I remind myself, biting my lip. *You're being watched!*

I bob her a curtsey. "Yes, ma'am."

Nigel's just standing there, being tweedy. But there's a big fat smirk on his face. He's loving every minute of this. He's the young master, with a Rabble at his beck and call!

"And tell her to wash that dirty face, Mamma," he whines. He's living dangerously. Wait until those cameras stop filming.

"And this time, make haste!" snaps the mistress. She keeps throwing smug looks at the camera in the corner, as if she's saying, "I know how to keep servants in their place."

"I did try to be quick, mistress."

I sound so polite it's sickening but she screams, "Don't answer me back, girl! Servants should be silent and obedient!"

I go galloping back down the stairs in my big, sloppy boots. I feel like shouting out something really rude to relieve my feelings. But I daren't. You never know who's listening.

This bucket of coal weighs a tonne. And I've got to lug it up three flights of stairs. What does she think I am, The World's Strongest Woman? I wonder how many slaveys dropped dead of overwork?

Squeak, squeak, squeak, squeak. What's that? It's my Victorian button-up boots. Now they're squeaking as well as clumping. They sound like a monster mouse.

At last I drag the coal bucket into the parlour. I'm nearly on my knees! But the mistress doesn't even say thanks. She's lounging on a red velvet sofa reading a magazine about embroidery. She says, "Well, put it on the fire, Raddle," without even bothering to look at me.

Nigel's whiny voice comes again. "And use the tongs. We don't want your hands making our coal dirty."

"I trust you gave it a good polish," chips in Nigel's mum.

"Eh?" I know the Victorians were dead keen on dusting and cleaning and scrubbing. I know servants even had to iron newspapers. But polishing coal? Is she winding me up?

I'm nearly biting my tongue off when the mistress makes up another order.

"A pot of tea, Raddle!" she cries. "For me and the young master."

"And make it quick!" says Nigel.

I race down the stairs and whizz round that kitchen like a whirlwind. Cups, saucers, teapot. It takes ages for the big copper kettle to boil. I go plodding back up three flights with a tray of wobbly tea things.

Squeak, clomp, squeak, clomp. Shut up, you boots.

"How slow you are, Raddle!" snaps the mistress.

Can't I do *anything* right?

"Don't you think we need more coal, Mamma?" says Nigel, with a cruel smile. He can't believe his luck. He's probably thinking, *A Rabble at my command! What can I make her do next?*

This time, I have to crawl up the stairs with that coal bucket. I'm panting and red-faced. I think I'm going to pass out. I'd give anything for a little lie-down. But that bell's got a shrill ring like it's shouting, *Hurry up! Hurry up!* I can't stand it, it's torture. And I've only been a slavey for half an hour.

Brrring! Brrring!

"All right, shut up, I'm coming!" I daren't say it out loud, of course. Just inside my head.

Phew, I nearly didn't make it that time. I'm practically collapsing! I stagger across the parlour, *squeak, clump, squeak* and dump the bucket of coals in front of the fire.

"What noisy boots!" says the mistress, looking up from her magazine. "You're making my head ache. In polite society, servants shouldn't be heard at all."

"Servants should be invisible!" says Nigel, the young master. "Then we wouldn't have to *see* them. *Ahh,*" he adds, cupping a hand round his ear, "do I hear the door chimes?"

Here we go again. I clatter downstairs three at a time, but when I open the front door there's nobody there. That creep Nigel. I knew he didn't hear anything.

Brinnng! There's that bell again. What do they want now? I'm cursing under my breath. I'm creeping upstairs, trying not to creak or clump, when Nigel slides out from behind a pot plant.

"I've seen you!" he cries, with this look of horror on his face, as if I'm something slimy he's found under a stone. "You're not trying hard enough to be invisible."

For heaven's sake! I flatten myself against a wall and start sliding along. Maybe he'll think I'm part of the wallpaper. Then I dodge into a doorway. Am I invisible enough? I peek out. Has he gone?

"I can still see you!" he cries. "Mamma, how frightful, I've *seen* a common person!"

Let's get this straight. I'm supposed to work myself to death waiting on them and be invisible at the same time? What kind of deal is that?

I dive under a little round table, and sit scrunched up, making myself as small as possible.

I'm starting to feel like a non-person, being ordered about, not allowed to make a sound. I'm not even allowed to be seen! What am I supposed to do with my body?

I think the young master's gone. It's safe to a make a run for it.

Brinng!

"I'm coming. I'm coming," I groan, under

my breath. "Don't get your bloomers in a twist."

I go skidding into the parlour. Great, I got here without the young master seeing me.

"You rang?" I gasp.

The mistress comes sweeping towards me with her dress crackling and her jewellery jangling. How come she can make all that racket but I can't? How come she can take up about a hundred times more space than me? Is it just because she's rich? She glowers at me, like I'm a bad smell under her nose.

"I hope my boots didn't disturb you, madam?"

"*Something* was creaking," says Nigel, who suddenly pops up in the doorway. "Perhaps it was her knees. From all that kneeling down and scrubbing. Servants aren't allowed to have creaky knees," he says severely.

"Perhaps it was her corsets," the mistress joins in. Now they're both ganging up on me and I've just got to stand here and take it. "You must oil them instantly," she orders. "Servants aren't allowed to have creaky corsets."

"I can't oil my corsets, ma'am."

For a split-second the mistress looks shocked. Am I daring to disobey an order?

"'Cos I'm not wearing any," I explain quickly, before she freaks out.

"*WHAT?*" The mistress seems to swell up like a black bouncy castle. She's shuddering with disgust. What have I done now?

"*NOT WEARING ANY CORSETS?*" she thunders in an outraged voice that makes the teacups tinkle. "I've never, ever heard anything so SCANDALOUS in my whole life! RESPECTABLE girls always wear corsets!"

She slumps back on the sofa with a hand to her forehead, "No corsets! I'm fainting from the sheer horror of it!"

Talk about overacting for the cameras! "I'll go and put some on immediately, ma'am."

But as I slink past her she grabs my arm. "Oh, no you don't!" She lowers her voice to a whisper so the cameras can't hear her. "Listen, you Rabble brat," she hisses, right in my face. What happened to her posh Victorian voice? "Tell me where the toilet is in this place. I'm dying to go. And I can't find one anywhere!"

"That's because the Victorians disguised toilets as something else."

"What as? Tell me, quick!"

I shrug. "It could be anything, really."

On my way down the stairs, I can hear her going from room to room hunting for the hidden toilet. She must be desperate. She's flinging furniture around! I think she's forgotten we're being filmed.

"It's not in this cupboard. Look in the piano stool, Nigel! Hurry up! Is it disguised as a bookcase? Or a coal scuttle?"

"*Heh, heh, heh,*" I'm chuckling to myself. It feels like I'm finally fighting back. I'm sick of being bossed about. Sick of being a slavey. And I've suddenly had an idea. Rupert's a member of The Early Rising Society. Well, I'm going to join a society of my own.

Brinng! Brinng! goes the bell. *Hurry up!*

But I'm not obeying orders any more.

Brinng! Brinng!

"Shut up, bell!" I tell it. "I'm revolting!"

The last thing I do, as I rush out the house to FREEDOM, is rip the horrible thing right out of the wall.

Chapter Ten

"I'm revolting, Dad!" I tell him. "I refuse to know my place!"

"But is this society you've just told me about authentic, Rae?" Dad asks me, looking worried.

"Yes, Dad. It really existed. I read about it."

If my voice sounds strange it's because I'm

holding my nose. You can tell Dad's been hanging out with Gilbert.

"Where is Gilbert, by the way?" I ask him.

"He's gone off somewhere with Rupert," says Dad. "I hope they aren't too long. I feel a bit of a fool being a pig man without a pig. People won't know what I'm supposed to be." He smoothes down his costume. "Should this smock stick out so much, Rae? Maybe I shouldn't have starched it. I feel like a giant traffic cone."

"*Shhh*, Dad. You can't say traffic cone. That's not very Victorian!"

"It's OK," says Dad. "That mike is too far away to pick up what I'm saying."

I'm really glad to be out on the street and not shut up in that dark gloomy house. There's loads happening here. It's so busy and bustling. Piemen and pickpockets and posh people all mixing together.

There are cameras everywhere. But I don't mind that. I want them to see me making my protest. I was never going to win that two hundred pounds being a slavey. No one notices a slavey.

Rupert comes dodging through the crowd.

He's still clutching his brush. He can't have done much sweeping up. It still looks as good as new.

I want to ask him about Mum's advert. I can't see it anywhere. Her sign should be fixed to a wall, where the cameras can see it. But Dad gets his question in first.

"Where's Gilbert? I thought he was with you."

"Oh, he's just drying off," says Rupert mysteriously.

In his other hand, Rupert's carrying an open can of red paint with a brush stuck in it.

"Hey, can I borrow that paint?" I dash round the back of the shops. It's not Victorian round here. And there are no cameras. But there's a plastic bin stuffed with cardboard. Just what I need.

It only takes a few minutes of painting. Then I go marching out into the street, pushing my way through the crowd, holding my placard high. It says, in big red letters, FREEDOM FROM CORSETS. NOW!

I make sure I'm standing slap bang in front of the house. I hope the mistress and the young master are spying out of the windows. If they're not, they soon will be.

Time to start shouting. "FREE WOMEN FROM THE SLAVERY OF CORSETS! FREE WOMEN FROM THE SLAVERY OF CORSETS!"

"Hey, Rae," says Rupert, running up. "What's all the noise about?"

"I'm standing up for my rights."

"Cool," says Rupert.

"I'm a militant member of The Anti-Lacing Society. We think tight corsets are a very BAD THING. They make you faint. You can't bend over in the middle. And they squeeze your insides to strawberry jam."

"Yuck," says Rupert. "You should fine people for wearing them then. Like The Early Rising Society fines people for staying in bed."

He dashes off again. Where's he going to now? He doesn't seem to be doing much sweeping.

Good old Dad. I'm making a big fuss. I'm causing loads of trouble but he's really proud.

"Excellent, Rae," he encourages me. "This is what Rent-a-Rabble is all about. *The Drama's in the Detail!* And The Anti-Lacing Society is a detail not many people know about."

"Well, they know about it now!"

A posh lady passes by, looking shocked. "Girls should be at home being sunbeams. Not raising their voices out on the streets!"

Everyone's staring. People are crowding round. I can see the curtains twitching in the house. Nigel and his mum must have finally figured out that their slavey got sick of taking orders.

"WE WANT FREEDOM FROM CORSETS! WHEN DO WE WANT IT? NOW!"

"'Ello! 'Ello! 'Ello! What's all this then?"

Oh, dear, somebody's sent for the police. I bet I know who that was.

The policeman looks familiar. He comes stomping through the crowd in his top hat and coat with shiny brass buttons. He looks like King Kong squeezed into a Victorian policeman's uniform. Only it isn't King Kong. It's Raymond.

Whoops. I forgot about him.

"Rabble!" he shouts. "Get back in that house! You've got loads of coal to polish!"

"Arrest her, Constable!" someone screams from the house window. I'd know that spiteful little voice anywhere.

Someone's tugging my arm. It's Ryan. Where's he been?

"Raymond's got the wrong top hat," he's babbling. "He picked up my new improved top hat by mistake. And I haven't finished making the modifications!"

"I haven't got time for your stupid inventions now," I hiss at him. "I'm protesting."

It's my big moment. I'm just about to be arrested. I'd better get that two hundred pound prize after all this brilliant acting.

But why is the crowd turning round? They've seen something else.

"*Oink!*"

A big, blubbery, black-and-pink thing comes galloping up the street. It's Gilbert, the historical pig. And what's that he's got painted on one side of his gigantic bottom in great, red letters?

"CROPPER AND CROUCH" it says.

Oh, no! I hope Mum hasn't logged on.

She's going to have a fit! Her firm's really snooty and high class. But it's being advertised on a fat, smelly pig's bottom. That isn't at all tasteful.

Especially since Gilbert just had a little accident in the street. A big accident, actually.

"Phew!" The whole crowd is holding their noses.

"Crossing sweeper!" bawls Constable Raymond. He just loves bullying people and being important. "Sweep up this mess!"

Rupert slopes up. He's got Rebel with him. He's beaming with pride. "Did you see my pig advert, Rae? In 1870, this guy advertised his bacon shop on a real *live* pig. He took it for walks round the town. It's a great idea isn't it, a walking advert! You could paint them on cows or horses. Or put teeny-weeny adverts on cockroaches. Course, I would never advertise bacon on Gilbert's bottom 'cos that would really upset him. Pigs have got feelings too—"

"Rupert," I interrupt him, "Mum's going to kill you!"

"But it's authentic!" protests Rupert.

I thought Rebel was going to keep Rupert out of trouble. But Rebel waggles his eyebrows at me, as if to say, "What do you think I am? Superdog? There's *no* way I can keep this weirdo under control."

"There's another authentic Victorian advert on his other side!" says Rupert proudly. "Do a twirl, Gilbert!"

"*OINK!*"

Gilbert turns round like a big wobbly jelly on tiny trotters.

"See," says Rupert. "That pig understands every word I say."

I read out the red letters on Gilbert's left cheek. "I *DIDN'T* TAKE DR PINKHAM'S SLIMMING PILLS."

"Mum's not going to like that, either," I tell Rupert. She's just going to hate her firm being advertised on the same pig's bottom as slimming pills. "You want to pray she's not logging on."

"Stop talking, you two! Sweep up this mess!" bawls Raymond again. He's got a puzzled scowl on his face. People usually do what he says straight away.

"Have you got belly-button fluff between

your ears!" yells Rupert. He seems to have forgotten we're being Victorian. And that he's talking to Raymond, Master of Menace. "I'm not going to get my lovely little broom all dirty with pig poo!"

Raymond's face, under his policeman's top hat, is going a scary shade of purple. That means he's getting mad. "Just do it, Rupert," I beg him. "Or we're mincemeat."

"No!" yells Rupert. Raymond grabs for the broom. Rupert holds on to it. They wrestle. For a minute I think Rupert's going to win. But Raymond's big bear paws snatch his broom away.

"My broom!" cries Rupert, heartbroken. "Give it back, you bully!"

But Raymond gives an evil sneer. Then he snaps Rupert's broom over his knee just like a matchstick.

Oh, dear, I'm thinking. *He shouldn't have done that.*

"*Aaaargh!*" screams Rupert. "You've broken it!" He goes berserk! He's wild with grief and rage. He hurls himself at Raymond. Rebel joins in. "*Grrr!*" He's tugging at Raymond's trousers.

But Rupert's weedy little body is clinging to Raymond's back like a monkey. He's kicking him with bare feet. Raymond probably doesn't even feel it.

Nigel comes strutting importantly out of the house. "Constable, have you arrested that Rabble yet?"

His mum sweeps out after him. She's making so much noise, in her crackly black dress and clanking jewellery, that no one can ignore her.

Where did she get that horrible hat? It's about the same size as our dustbin lid. And those big feathers are really over the top. It looks like a dead ostrich has been dumped on her head.

"Arrest all those Rabbles!" she orders Raymond in her haughtiest voice. "They are a public nuisance! They shouldn't be allowed on the same street as RESPECTABLE people!"

Rupert has got his skinny arms wrapped around Raymond's neck. I think he wants to strangle him. It's a bit like trying to choke a tree trunk to death. But Rupert won't give in. "You – big – bully! You – broke – my – broom!"

Raymond doesn't look at all bothered – it's as if a butterfly has landed on him.

Desperately, my brother dangles off Raymond's neck with all his weight. Something's happening. Raymond's neck bends back a few centimetres.

"No!" Ryan shouts out a warning. "Let go, Rupert. Don't force his head back! His top hat will think he's being garrotted!"

Too late. The top of the hat flies opens. "HELP! HELP!" a voice shrieks from inside. "My master is being robbed!"

"Eh?" growls Raymond, spinning around with Rupert – and Rebel – still hanging on. "Who said that? I didn't say that!"

But the hat has only just started. When Ryan invents something his brain doesn't know when to stop.

Whoosh! A rocket comes whizzing out of Raymond's top hat. It zigzags down the street, spitting red fire.

"Duck!" The muffin man hurls himself to the floor. His muffins go rolling over the cobbles.

"Look out!" People are diving into shop doorways!

The rocket bounces off a shop sign, shoots up into the air, then *BOOM!* it splits into a thousand stars.

"There goes the distress flare," says Ryan, as if we might have missed it. "I didn't think that would work."

Raymond's staggering about, holding his ears. "My head's just exploded!" Rupert's still hanging on, like a human backpack. He's being joggled about. But he won't let go.

"You broke my broom!"

There's chaos in the street. "Fire!" shouts the lady selling lavender. Some people have already starting running.

"HELP! HELP!" The hat's shrieking non-stop, making everyone even more hysterical.

It's like a magician's top hat at parties. There's more and more stuff coming out of it! Except it's not doves or paper flowers. It's thick, black, stinking smoke.

"Here comes the smoke screen," says Ryan coolly, like he's giving a running commentary. "It's to confuse his attackers. And give him the chance to escape. . ."

"Help, help!" the hat shrieks, as a black cloud swirls down the street.

"Is that smoke coming from *me*?" shouts Raymond.

Loud bells start clanging. People are stumbling about. "Where's the way out?" There's mass panic!

"Oh, dear," says Ryan, from somewhere in the smelly black smoke. "I think I've set off the smoke alarms."

Rupert slides off Raymond's back, coughing. I'm coughing too. This smoke's really smelly and thick. I can't see a thing –

"*Ruff!*" I think I've tripped over Rebel. What's that I'm sliding about in?

Then suddenly I'm soaked! I'm gasping as cold water comes hissing down. How can it be raining? We're indoors!

Ryan's voice says, sounding slightly surprised, "There's a sprinkler system. That's a pity. It'll put my hat out."

The smoke's clearing. Now, I can see something. The last few people in soggy costumes are fighting their way out of the exit. That's not very Victorian. What happened to being polite?

"*Oink!*" Gilbert gallops by. The adverts are washing off his bottom in a river of red.

"Wait for me!" Rupert races after him. Now his broom's broken, Gilbert is his best friend.

Nigel's mum's ostrich feathers have had a disaster. Instead of standing up stiff, they're dangling dripping wet down her neck.

"Come, Nigel!"

She flounces off. But it's hard to look toffee-nosed when you're squelching water with every step.

"I bet you Rabbles are behind all this!" sneers Nigel.

"Clear off, creep!"

"I'll get Raymond to give you a jolly good thumping!" threatens Nigel. But he says it from a safe distance – then scurries off after his mum. His minder's not much use at the moment.

Raymond's wandering about, looking dazed. "I've got these voices in me head!" The top hat is a total wreck. It looks like he's wearing a giant burnt-out firework.

"Heelp, heeeeeelp." What's happening to the hat's cry for help? It goes all deep and drawly. Then suddenly stops.

"Tut, tut, I was afraid that would happen,"

says Ryan. "The tape's got damaged. There's a tiny cassette player inside, you know."

How many things can you cram into one top hat?

"Is there a kitchen sink in there as well?" I ask Ryan, trying to be clever.

Ryan just looks at me as if I'm really dumb and replies, "No, Rae, you'd have to have a much bigger top hat than that to fit a kitchen sink in." Why can't my family ever understand sarcasm?

Raymond goes staggering towards the exit.

"Hey! He's stealing my top hat," says Ryan, chasing after him. "That's my best, most brilliant invention yet. It'll work like a dream – with a few minor modifications. . ."

That leaves Dad and me and Rebel alone, in an empty street. We're all drenched. Rebel shakes himself in a shower of spray.

He shoots me a look. As if to say, "And you humans think you're the superior species? Do me a favour!"

Dad's paper hat has sort of dissolved. It's like white sludge stuck to his hair. The starch has washed out of his smock. It's all clingy, like a wet T-shirt. "Aren't you wearing any underwear, Dad? That's disgusting!"

I should know what he's going to answer.

"I'm only being authentic, Rae. The poor people Rent-a-Rabble play couldn't afford underwear."

"That's no excuse! They could have borrowed a pair of Queen Victoria's bloomers."

I sound more hysterical than Ryan's top hat. I've got to get a grip. You'd think I'd be used to everything going pear-shaped with Rent-a-Rabble.

It's suddenly gone awfully silent. The fire alarms have stopped. Dad spits out some water. "Thank goodness for some peace and quiet."

Then six fire engines come screaming through the museum gates. . .

We're in the Rent-a-Rabble van, squeezing water out of our rags. We're on the way home. Victorian Day is a write-off. The street has got to be dried out. All of the expensive cameras and recording equipment are ruined.

Ryan doesn't seem to have a clue about

the trouble he's caused. He's still babbling on about his invention.

"It was a mercury switch, right? And as soon as Raymond's head tilted back, *pow*, everything happened! The mercury completed the electrical circuit that made a spark that lit the distress flare that ignited the old socks soaked in oil. That was why the smoke was so black and stinky!" He says it like it's something to be really proud of.

"I wish I could've got it back," he says sadly. "But that Raymond ran off with it."

I'm hopping mad. "Dad! Tell him off, Dad! He's spoiled everything."

We haven't won any prizes. We're probably not even going to get paid.

At first Dad seems to back me up. "Actually, Ryan," he says, severely, from the driving seat. "That hat was extremely dangerous. Things igniting on people's heads are *not* a good idea. Raymond might have been badly hurt."

"But the hat was fireproof, Dad!" protests Ryan.

Then Dad lets me down. "That smoke was

a very authentic detail though," he can't help adding. "Just like a Victorian pea-souper."

"A what?"

"In towns they had frightful, stinking fogs called pea-soupers caused by all the smoke from factories. And I must say, Ryan, you recreated that very well—"

"Dad!" I say despairingly. "You're *supposed* to be telling him off. Not making him feel good! It's his fault we're not getting paid – again!"

"Actually," shrugs Ryan, "if Rupert hadn't tried to strangle Raymond that hat would have behaved itself. It would have been as good as gold."

"I only tried to strangle him because he broke my lovely little broom!"

"Hey, stop, Dad!" shouts Ryan suddenly, peering out the van window. "There's my hat!"

It's got Raymond underneath it. He's squelching along the road, looking dazed. He's still wearing his Victorian policeman's uniform.

"Let's give him a lift," says Dad.

Me and Rupert object. "You must be

joking!" says Rupert. "I don't want that broom-mangler in here!"

"Don't tell me you feel sorry for him, Dad!" I shout out.

That's Dad's trouble. He feels sorry for all sorts of dodgy people – even for Raymond. He stops the van. "Jump in, son," he says.

Raymond grunts and climbs in. He doesn't seem to notice he's in a van full of Rabbles. He just slumps in a seat and goes totally silent.

"That exploding top hat has messed up his brain," I whisper to Rupert.

"He didn't have a brain to mess up in the first place!" raves Rupert. He's still really upset about that broom. He's got the bits of it in the van with him. He's already said, "I want to bury them in the garden." He looks ready to leap on Raymond all over again.

Now Rebel's growling. "Stop it, you two," I warn them. We don't want a big fight here in the van. We might crash. We might all end up in hospital wearing Queen Victoria's bloomers. Why do I keep thinking about them? That's seriously strange.

Then Dad interrupts. What he says stops us all squabbling. "Brace yourselves, kids!" he warns us. "We're home. Mum's waiting in the drive. *And she doesn't look happy!*"

Did Dad say Mum doesn't look happy? That's the understatement of the year. Mum looks like a volcano that's about to blow.

As soon as we stop, Rupert sneaks out. "*M'i ffo!*"

"*Ruff!*" says Rebel, trotting off after him. They can see there's trouble ahead.

Without a word, Raymond climbs out the van. Ryan whips the top hat off his head: "Mine, I think!" Raymond doesn't even notice. He goes plodding off down the road. Does he know his way home? He looks like a zombie. I told Dad off just now for feeling sorry for him. I can hardly believe it, but I feel a teeny bit sorry for him too.

But I don't have time to worry about Raymond now. Mum's on the warpath.

"Where's Rupert?" she's yelling, rushing up to meet me and Dad. "I'm going to kill him! I logged on and there was this pig, with the name of my firm painted on its bottom, doing something disgusting. Then Rupert started a fight. And then it turned into a disaster movie! Rockets whizzing everywhere! People rushing around screaming in the smoke. Then getting half-drowned. Then my computer screen went completely blank! What on earth was going on?"

Dad looks nervous. "Well, dear," he starts off, picking a bit of paper sludge out of his hair, "Victorian Day didn't go exactly according to plan—"

Suddenly, Rupert comes running out of the house. "Mum! Mum!" he's shouting.

I thought he was going to keep out of Mum's way. He's going straight up to her! Has he got a death wish? But there's a big, beaming grin fixed to his face. Is he trying to break his smiling record?

"Mum!" he yells. "This posh woman just rung me up. And guess what? I'm famous! I've won an award!"

Chapter Eleven

It's not fair. What is it about Rupert? One minute he's in deep disgrace. And the next he's everyone's favourite person.

Back in the house, Dad explains. "Do you remember when Rupert was getting in the Victorian mood? And he went to the park to collect—?"

"I'd rather forget about that, thank you," I

interrupt him. I can't even *look* at a super-market carrier bag any more without feeling sick.

Rebel says *"Ruff!"* from under the table. He doesn't want to remember it either. Rebel likes to roam wild and free. Having Rupert following him round with a shovel really cramped his style.

"But this woman saw me," says Rupert. "And she's a Very Important Person."

"A councillor," adds Dad, "who lives in a big house that overlooks the park."

Rupert can't wait to take over. He's wriggling about with excitement. "Yeah! And when she saw me she thought, 'How wonderful that a young person cares about cleaning up our environment.' She thought, 'That young man deserves our *Caring Young Citizen of the Year Award.*' So she found out who I was—"

"But you didn't do it to be a caring young citizen," I butt in. "You were practising to be a Victorian dog-dirt collector."

"I know," says Rupert, looking sly. "But she doesn't, does she?"

"Very well done," says Mum proudly. She

seems to have forgotten that Rupert painted the name of her firm on a pig's bottom.

"And it'll be great publicity," adds Dad. Rupert's news has really cheered him up after the Victorian Day disaster. "He's bound to get interviewed by the press."

"I might even get on telly!" says Rupert.

"But whenever you get interviewed, son, be sure to get in a mention for Rent-a-Rabble," says Dad.

"Right, Space Captain, sir," says Rupert, saluting.

Rebel and me exchange looks. We're both thinking the same thing – that Rupert must have been born under a lucky star.

I'd never heard of it, but the *Caring Young Citizen of the Year Award* turns out to be a really big deal. I'd be embarrassed, getting an award for being a champion pooper-scooper. My mates would never let me live it down. But Rupert just loves it – all the inter-views and the photographs and the fame. He's getting all the attention he ever dreamed of.

And there's another thing that makes him happy. "I bet the award is a big load of money!" he says, his eyes gleaming. "I might even get enough to buy Gilbert!"

We're all there, on the day Rupert gets his prize. We're down in the audience, in our best clothes. Dad did think about turning up in peasants' rags to get more publicity for Rent-a-Rabble. He thought about it for two seconds. Until Mum said, "Over my dead body!"

Rupert is up there, in a special seat on the platform, surrounded by very important people. He looks dead smart; he's got his hair slicked down with gel.

Her Worshipful the Mayor is next to him. In front of him is the Chief Constable, the top policeman, wearing a very posh uniform, all glittery with gold braid. There are reporters from newspapers, photographers with flashbulbs popping. Even local telly is filming. Like I said, it's a big deal. Everything is turning out really well. And I haven't thought about Queen Victoria's bloomers for ages.

Oh, rats.

Her Worshipful the Mayor comes to the front. She drones on about the award. And at last she says, "And here is our *Caring Young Citizen,* Rupert Rabble!"

We clap until our hands hurt. Rupert trots up to the front trying to look modest.

"And here is your prize," says Her Worshipful. "You should be very proud of it."

It's a certificate. Just a crummy old bit of white cardboard. My first thought is, *There's going to be trouble.* And beside me, I can hear Mum sighing, "Oh, dear."

Rupert can't believe it either. He turns the certificate over, in case there's some money stuck to the back. He stands there, waiting for something else.

"You may sit down now, Rupert," smiles Her Worshipful. Rupert's bottom lip slides out like a fat, pink slug.

We all recognize the warning signs. What's he going to do next? You can never be sure with Rupert. He might chuck the certificate away. He might stamp on it. He might shout out something really rude, like, "You know where you can stick this!"

We're all holding our breaths. Except Ryan, who's sketching some plans on his hand. Maybe it's his top hat, Mark III. But Rupert turns round, clutching the certificate, and trudges to his seat. His droopy shoulders show that he's really fed up.

"*Phew!*" says Dad, wiping his forehead. Like me, he's amazed. He thought Rupert was going to make a scene.

Maybe Rupert caught Mum's eye. We're six rows back in the audience. But Mum's look could shrivel you from miles away.

I thought the award ceremony would be over by now. The sooner we get Rupert out of here, the better. But it drags on for ages. How many more people are going to make speeches?

Rupert's getting restless. He's yawning, great, big, jaw-cracking yawns. Now he's kicking his shoes against the chair. He's rolling his certificate into a tube and spying at us through it.

Then, in the row in front of Rupert, the Chief Constable takes off his peaked cap. He must be getting too hot. His head is glittering under the lights. My stomach does a crash-dive. Because it's the biggest, bumpiest, baldest head I've ever seen. . .

Rupert's seen it too. He couldn't miss it. It's right under his nose. His eyes light up, like a crocodile that's seen its dinner. He can't take his eyes off that tempting bonce. He's hypnotized! He throws his certificate away. His arms stretch out, like a praying mantis. His fingers are twitching.

He isn't going to, is he?

He isn't going to have a really good feel of the Chief Constable's head? And then shout out, "This man's a criminal!"

"Yes, he is!" gasps Dad, reading my mind.

"Rupert! No!" we yell, like one person, as we both burst out of our seats and go racing towards the platform.